The Right Amount of Sunshine…
Cultivating Little Girls into Young Ladies

Companion Journal

————————————————'s

(Your Name Here)

Journal

Rule #1:

THERE ARE NO RULES!

This is **YOUR** Journal!

You can write wherever, doodle wherever, or glue photos wherever!

You can choose to answer a prompt, or not!

And in whatever order you choose!

This is your safe place, so be you and let it all out!

Shine On…

Brenda's Child

Why Do You Shine?
What makes you stand out?
What about you is unique?
How do you know?

Date:

Support

Who makes up your support system? Who shows up? Who can you count on and why? (If the answer is "No One'" write about why? How can you begin to seek out positive sources of support?)

Talent

What special talents do you have? Which talents would you like to develop and how can you go about doing so? How confident are you that you could turn your talents in a career?

Date:

Struggle

Compare yourself to an animal when faced with confrontation or struggle. Think about what might influence you to respond that way?

Date:

_____

_____

_____

_____

_____

_____

_____

_____

_____

_____

_____

_____

_____

_____

_____

_____

_____

_____

_____

_____

_____

_____

_____

_____

_____

_____

_____

_____

_____

_____

Bullying

Reflect on a time when you've been bullied, a bully, or a bystander.
First think about how you felt in that position, then try to imagine what was going on in the mind and heart of the other person?

Date:

Friendship

What qualities make a good
friend? What qualities do
you dislike in a friend? Do
you honestly feel that you
are a good friend to others?
In which area can you
improve?

Jealousy vs Envy

Now that you know the difference between jealousy and envy, write about a time you felt either or both. Also, write about a time someone was jealous or envious of you? How did you know? Do you think you understand why this person felt this way?

Date:

Fights and Drama

Think about a fight or an argument you had with a friend. Reflect on the fight from another angle, either from the other person's point of view, or from hindsight (knowledge or understanding you have gained.)

Date:

Shadows

Do you ever feel like you are living in someone else's shadow (a sibling, friend, or family member?) Or are you just hiding in your own shadows? What's preventing you from stepping out into the sunlight?

<u>Boys</u>

Have you ever pretended to be something you weren't because you liked a boy, or done something out of the ordinary to impress one?

Childhood

When you were younger, what were some of your favorite toys and games? Did you ever make up your own games?

_____
_____
_____
_____
_____
_____
_____
_____
_____
_____
_____
_____
_____
_____
_____
_____
_____
_____
_____
_____
_____
_____
_____
_____
_____
_____

Breaking the Out of the Box

Date:

Reflect on a time when someone tried to limit you because of who you are. (Where you come from, your race, culture or religion, gender, or age). How did it make you feel? How did you respond?

_____

_____

_____

_____

_____

_____

_____

_____

_____

_____

_____

_____

_____

_____

_____

_____

_____

_____

_____

_____

_____

_____

_____

_____

_____

_____

Self-Acceptance

Date:

Do you know who you are? If so, how accepting of it are you, despite what people say?

Role Models

Different people influence us in different areas of our lives; the way we dress, our careers, our education, our spiritual beliefs, and our relationships with others. Who are your female role models and why? These can be celebrities, but also think about women you know. What about them inspires you?

Dad

Whether he's living or not, a major part of your life or someone you've never met, write an honest letter to your father discussing your feelings for him, positive and/or negative.

Pain

People deal with loss and emotional pain differently. What are some ways (good or bad) you cope with loss and emotional pain? If any are them are negative, list some more positive ways you can try.

Spirituality

Date:

What do you think happens to us when we die? Where do these beliefs come from? How does that make you feel?

_____
_____
_____
_____
_____
_____
_____
_____
_____
_____
_____
_____
_____
_____
_____
_____
_____
_____
_____
_____
_____
_____
_____
_____
_____
_____
_____
_____
_____

Saying Goodbye

Date:

Write a letter to someone whom you felt you never got to say goodbye to for whatever reason.

Memories

If you've ever lost someone to death, write about some positive ways you can honor their memory and keep it alive.

Your Body

Describe what you love most about your body

Body Image

Whose body shape do you admire most and why? Where or whom did this idea about what is attractive come?

_____
_____
_____
_____
_____
_____
_____
_____
_____
_____
_____
_____
_____
_____
_____
_____
_____
_____
_____
_____
_____
_____
_____
_____
_____
_____

Puberty

As your body has changed, are there things that you've tried to enhance, to hide, make bigger or smaller? Why? If not, what reason do you think you haven't?

Compliments and Insults

Most of the time we remember the negative comments more than the positive. Below list the five worst insults people have said to you. Underneath them, re-write the insult as a compliment.

Example:

Insult:

Eww...you have stretch marks!

Compliment:

I am meant to stretch beyond any limits set for me.

Place full body photo of yourself with today's date here:

Experimenting with Danger

Date:

Write about a time you put yourself in physical danger by doing something risky, that you knew you shouldn't do, but did it anyway. What influenced your decision? Do you regret doing it, or was there something you learned?

_____
_____
_____
_____
_____
_____
_____
_____
_____
_____
_____
_____
_____
_____
_____
_____
_____
_____
_____
_____
_____
_____
_____

Leader or Follower?

Date:

Within your circle of friends would you say that you are a leader or a follower? How do you know? Depending on your role, have you been peer pressured or peer pressured someone? What was your motivation for it? (What were you hoping to gain?

Choices

Date:

Who do you think influences
your choices about
experimenting with drugs
and alcohol the most?
(Parents, friends, religion,
the media, fear, past
experience).

Love

Date:

What does it mean to love someone? Is there a difference between loving someone and being in love with someone?

In Love

Date:

Have you ever been in love? If not, what is your idea of what it should look like?

Virginity

Write some of your thoughts about virginity? How important is it to you and why? If you are still a virgin, how do you think you will know when the time is right? If you are no longer a virgin, reflect on your decision to "yield" it to someone. If it was "taken" from you, write about how you can "reclaim it" in your own way.

Date:

Questions?

Date:

Write down a list of questions you have about sex or things you're unsure about. Seek the answers from a trusted adult, or visit www.myshineon.info for links to trusted websites.

Confidence
When do you feel most confident?

Date:

_____
_____
_____
_____
_____
_____
_____
_____
_____
_____
_____
_____
_____
_____
_____
_____
_____
_____
_____
_____
_____
_____
_____
_____
_____
_____
_____
_____
_____
_____
_____
_____
_____
_____
_____
_____
_____
_____

Self-Esteem

How would rate your self-esteem on a scale of 1 to 10? Explain your response.

_____

_____

_____

_____

_____

_____

_____

_____

_____

_____

_____

_____

_____

_____

_____

_____

_____

_____

_____

_____

_____

_____

_____

_____

_____

_____

_____

_____

_____

_____

_____

_____

Music

Throughout the memoir, Brenda's Child mentions songs and lyrics during important parts of her life. What are some songs that are important to you and why?

_____
_____
_____
_____
_____
_____
_____
_____
_____
_____
_____
_____
_____
_____
_____
_____
_____
_____
_____
_____
_____
_____
_____
_____
_____
_____
_____
_____
_____

Random Thoughts

Place a photo here of whatever you'd like

Use The
Margin Space
For
Inspirational
Quotes

Made in the USA
Lexington, KY
10 February 2017